Groovy Girls™ Sleep Over Club

Sleepover Surprise
A Twin-sational Birthday

Robin Epstein

Scholastic Inc.

New York   Toronto   London   Auckland   Sydney
Mexico City   New Delhi   Hong Kong   Buenos Aires

Read all the books about the Groovy Girls!

To my big sister, Amy, the girl who taught me
to scoop poop with a smile!

Cover illustration by Taia Morley
Interior illustrations by Bill Alger, Doug Day,
Kurt Marquart, and Yancey Labat

ISBN 0-439-81433-2

12 11 10 9 8 7 6 5 4 3 2 1   5 6 7 8 9 10/0

Printed in the U.S.A.
First Little Apple printing, September 2005

"**S**hhhush!" Reese said loudly to her twin sister, O'Ryan, as the girls snooped through their mother's bedroom closet. "Do you *want* us to get caught?"

"Hey, it's not exactly like I was *trying* to make her shoe hit me on the head...then hit a box... then crash to the floor," O'Ryan replied.

"I don't get it! It's only three days till our birthday," Reese added, as she sifted through

Mom's sneakers, stacked heels, and ballerina flats. "So why can't we find our B-day presents?"

"I know. There should be LOTS of presents for us to find by now," O'Ryan responded.

Reese agreed. "Double digits should *definitely* mean double presents."

There was no doubt the girls were going to find their birthday treasures eventually.

After all, the twins were expert snoopers.

They could find a needle in a haystack (as long as that needle had "To O'Ryan and Reese" engraved on it).

In fact, each year the girls made a list of the gifts they thought they might be getting. And with that list, they could better imagine where their parents could hide something based on its size!

The list was made of three columns:

DEFINITE GETS	LIKELY POSSIBILITIES	NO WAY, IT'LL NEVER HAPPEN, BUT A GIRL CAN DREAM, CAN'T SHE?
🌼 Vintage t-shirts	🌼 Peacock feather earrings	🌼 Plane tickets to Alaska

"Wait a second!" Reese yelled. "I think I see something!" She reached her arm deep into the back of the closet. "What's this?"

Reese pulled out a small box with strawberry-print wrapping paper on it and a big silky bow.

"Shake it," O'Ryan instructed.

"Okay, that provided exactly zero info," Reese said. "I think we should investigate a little further."

Luckily, she was one crafty unwrapper!

She turned the strawberry-papered box over and slowly slid her finger under the seam to lift the tape. Once she'd successfully removed the paper, Reese opened the box top and the girls saw...

A pair of bulky, brown woolen socks?

"*What?*" O'Ryan said in disbelief.

Not only weren't these socks snazzy, they were a "zero" on the scale of groov-i-tude.

And, they were *E-normous*!

They were socks for Bigfoot.

"Wait a second," Reese said. "There's a card in here."

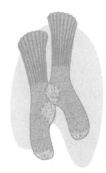

"Read it!" O'Ryan demanded.

"It says, 'Dear O'Ryan and Reese, nice try! But this *isn't* a gift for you.

It's for Grandma Gertie. So, please rewrap this present and put it back where you found it. Love, Mom.'"

"Got to hand it to her," O'Ryan admitted. "Mom's getting good."

"Thank you," Mom replied, walking into her bedroom and catching the twins mid-snoop.

"Oh, Mom! We were just—" Reese stammered.

"Yes, I can see that," Mom said, smiling. "I'm sorry to disappoint you, girls, but your gift isn't in here. In fact, it's not even in the house yet."

"Do you think she means it?" O'Ryan whispered to Reese as Mom left the room.

"No way," Reese replied, shaking her head. "She probably just said that to throw us off the trail."

"And if Mom and Dad are being so smart about this, we need to be, too," O'Ryan said. "We've gotta go back to our size-finder list."

But as she started walking out of their parents' room, Reese stopped her sister.

"Hey," Reese said, "we can't leave their room looking like this."

O'Ryan glanced around and saw that she and Reese had made quite a mess of things.

"Okay," O'Ryan said. "Let's get everything

cleaned up in here. Then let's hit the list."

The girls put everything back in place perfectly. They even did a little extra organizing to make up for getting caught.

When they were done, the twins ran back to their own room.

"Okay, first thing tomorrow we start searching the coat closet downstairs for boxes of clothes," Reese said.

"Right, and where would they hide a hair straightener?"

"Or a video game?"

"Or a puppy?"

"Or Rollerblades?"

The girls kept adding gift possibilities to their list, trying to figure out the perfect hiding place for each one. And even though they didn't really expect it, they didn't rule out the possibility that there'd be a cute little pink Corvette waiting for them in the garage when they looked there first thing tomorrow morning!

 **Vrooooommmmm!**

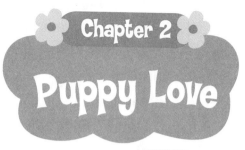

Chapter 2

Puppy Love

"Okay—who laid an egg?" O'Ryan asked as she and Reese walked into class the next morning.

"O'Ryan, don't be gross!" Reese giggled. "Maybe Mrs. Pearlman just wants us to have an *eggs-cellent* day."

Mysteriously, an egg sat in the pencil slot of each student's desk, with each of their initials on it.

And next to each egg, a tag read: HANDLE ME WITH CARE!

"Yay, breakfast!" Gwen yelled, seeing the eggs when she came running into the classroom a moment later. "I was running late—as usual—so I didn't get a chance to eat yet," she explained.

"Well, then eat up, Gwen," Oki replied. "'Cause you know what they say, 'an egg a day keeps the chickens away!'"

"Who says *that*?" O'Ryan asked.

But before Oki could give her *eggs*-planation, Mrs. P. entered the classroom.

"Good morning, class!" she said, carefully closing the door behind her. "Please take your seats...but do so ver-ry gent-ly!" she added, pointing to the eggs.

"Are we doing an egg toss?" O'Ryan asked. "That game is so fun!"

"No, O'Ryan," Mrs. Pearlman replied. "These eggs aren't for a game. They're for our next social studies unit. It's called 'Being a Responsible Citizen.'"

Oki rolled her eyes at O'Ryan, and O'Ryan's eyes rolled right back.

NOT fun, both girls thought.

"You see," Mrs. Pearlman continued, "being responsible is a big, important idea, and it means everything from doing homework, to taking out the garbage, to voting (when you're an adult), to taking care of our planet, and to caring for one another."

"So what does that have to do with eggs?" Reese asked.

"Well, when you take care of an egg, it can take care of you."

"You mean like giving us food?" Gwen said.

"Or more chickens?" Oki called out.

"Which means more food!" Gwen replied.

"That's right," Mrs. Pearlman said. "But to get the benefits from an egg, you need to handle it with care, right? Almost like it's a newborn baby. So for the next week, each of you will be responsible for taking care of the egg on your desk."

"So it's like our...egg baby?" O'Ryan asked.

"An egg baby?" Gwen repeated with delight. "Are you yolking?"

"Nope, no yolk!" Mrs. P. laughed. "Your assignment is to tend to that egg, making sure it doesn't crack or break. You'll have to watch it all the time, and take it with you everywhere you go."

"Wait. We're supposed to take our egg babies *everywhere*?" Reese asked.

"If you think about it, your parents are responsible for you twenty-four hours a day!

Being responsible is a full-time job," Mrs. P. said.

"But what if we have to do something where we can't be with them, Mrs. P.?" Oki called out.

"Well, class, what do parents do when they can't watch their children?"

"They turn on the TV set," O'Ryan replied. "Or, they get a babysitter, right?"

"Exactly. You find someone you trust to look after your child," Mrs. P. answered. "Because being a responsible citizen means making sure things are being taken care of."

"Sounds like a lot of work," Reese said.

"At first it may seem that way, Reese," Mrs. Pearlman said. "But hopefully, it will become second nature to you quickly. It's like getting to school on time. Or bringing in the mail. Or taking care of your little brother, or a pet."

Mrs. Pearlman opened the door to the classroom. "To teach us a little more about responsibility, I've invited a special guest to class today. She's right outside...Maggie?"

But Maggie didn't enter.

"Guess she's a little shy," Oki said to O'Ryan.

"Maggie, come on, girl!" Mrs. Pearlman repeated, this time slapping her hands against her thighs.

Everyone in the class looked around.

This seemed a weird way to talk to a guest!

Who is this mysterious Maggie girl?

And then came a jingling sound.

And a moment later, the mystery was solved!

Because Maggie, a bouncy, tan-colored cocker spaniel, came bounding into the classroom.

"Maggie's a doggy?" Reese asked excitedly.

And sure enough, tail wagging, body wiggling, and tongue hanging out, Maggie pranced up to the front of the classroom after Mrs. Pearlman.

"Is that your pooch, Mrs. P.?" O'Ryan asked.

"Yes, she is," Mrs. Pearlman replied, stroking the dog's ears.

"Look at how silky her coat is!" Oki said.

"She's so friendly," O'Ryan added.

"And happy!" Reese chimed in.

"And frisky!" Oki noted.

Gwen had gotten out of her chair, along with everyone else, when Maggie came into the class. But instead of going to the front of the room, she headed straight to the back.

"Is everything okay, Gwen?" Mrs. Pearlman

asked when she looked up.

"Uh, yeah, sorta," Gwen replied. "But, um, is that dog going to be here all day?"

"No," Mrs. Pearlman answered. "I'm taking her back home at lunch."

"Good," Gwen said under her breath. "Can I go to the nurse now? I'm not feeling so well."

"Of course you can," Mrs. Pearlman replied. "Here, take the hall pass." Mrs. P. walked over to her desk to get the fluorescent orange paddle. But when she started walking to the back of the classroom to hand it to Gwen, Maggie began to follow her.

"Maybe you can just throw it to me," Gwen said quickly.

Mrs. Pearlman nodded. "Reese, since you're closer to Gwen than I am, can you pass this to her?"

"Sure," Reese replied, taking the hall pass from Mrs. P. and walking it back to Gwen. "I hope you feel better," Reese said. "I didn't even *know* you were sick."

"It happened kind of suddenly," Gwen said. "I'm sure I'll feel better by lunch."

"Wait!" Reese cried out. "Don't forget your egg baby!"

"Oh, yeah," Gwen replied. She walked back over to her desk, and just as she was picking up her egg, Maggie barked. "WHOA!" Gwen said, fumbling with the egg. As soon as she got control of it again, she ran out of the classroom.

"So how come your dog's visiting on egg–baby day?" Oki asked.

"Because," Mrs. Pearlman replied, "my Maggie is about to have some babies of her own. And soon she'll have a whole litter of puppies to take care of. Which is what you call a whole lot of responsibility!"

"But Maggie and I can't take care of all of those pups ourselves. We're going to need some help."

"We can help!" Reese said. "We'll take a puppy home."

"That may be possible, but you'll need to talk about that with your parents first," replied Mrs. P.

"If we can get permission, we can get a pup?" asked O'Ryan.

"Well, not so fast. Your egg babies are also going to help me decide who'd be responsible enough to have a dog," said Mrs. Pearlman.

Huh?

"You see, at the end of this project," Mrs. P. explained, "you're all going to tell us about your experiences with your egg."

"Cool!" Oki said.

"In an essay," Mrs. Pearlman added.

"Less cool," Oki replied.

Reese looked at O'Ryan, and O'Ryan looked at Reese.

And they both knew *eggs-actly* what the other one was thinking.

It was: *I WANT A DOG*!!!

And suddenly both twins knew what they wanted for their birthday more than anything else.

More than a drum set.

More than a hair straightener.

More than a video game.

(Well, truth be told, they were still hoping to get all those things, too.)

But what they really, *really* wanted—more than *any*thing else—was something that didn't even come wrapped with a bow. What they wanted was: Parental Permission for a Pearlman Puppy!

Chapter 3

Cracking Up!

"Your egg baby's wearing a hair bow!" Reese exclaimed when she saw Gwen and her egg sitting at the table in the cafeteria. "How cute!"

"I made it with some gauze I got in the nurse's office," Gwen said, as Reese, O'Ryan, and Oki took their seats next to her.

"Very groovy, Gwen!" Oki nodded with approval, cradling her own egg in her hands.

"And practical!" Gwen grinned. "'Cause the gauze bow also doubles as a helmet, just in case Eggsmerelda—that's what I named her—falls!"

As the girls laughed, Vanessa and Yvette walked over to the table carrying their trays.

"Hey, careful!" O'Ryan exclaimed as the older girls put their trays down. "We don't want to make an omelet here!"

"Oh!" Vanessa said. "So you guys are doing the unit on Responsibility, huh?"

"We did that last year," Yvette added, taking her seat. "It was a good one."

"Are you feeling better?" Reese asked her best friend, Gwen, interrupting the other conversation.

"Much better!" Gwen answered. "Thanks."

Then she added: "I wasn't really feeling sick when I asked to go to the nurse."

"I *knew* you were faking!" O'Ryan said. "You went from zero to sickly pretty fast!"

"Hey, I wasn't *totally* faking," Gwen replied. "I mean I *did* have a stomach ache. I'm just not sure I want to tell you why."

"You can tell us," Reese said, leaning in.

"Well," Gwen hesitated. "Well…the truth is… my stomach hurt 'cause of Maggie."

"Maggie?" Vanessa repeated.

"Mrs. P. brought her dog to class," Reese explained to Vanessa and Yvette.

"You mean you were scared of Mrs. Pearlman's cocker spaniel?" Oki asked.

Gwen nodded. "Dogs freak me out."

"No kidding?" Reese asked. "I never knew that."

"Well, it's not *exactly* something I brag about," Gwen replied.

"That's so weird, 'cause I love dogs," Reese said. She just assumed if she adored dogs, her best friend would, too.

"We're going to try to convince our parents to let us have one of Mrs. Pearlman's puppies for our birthday!" O'Ryan said. "*Which*, by the way, is in exactly two—count 'em, *one, two*—days! Just so none of you forgets!"

"Oh, I'm sure you'll get a puppy for your birthday," Gwen replied.

"Why would you say something like that, Gwen?" Vanessa asked sharply.

"I mean you have to be pretty mature to take care of a dog," Yvette added quickly.

"We know." Reese frowned. "We've wanted one for practically forever. But our parents *always* say we aren't ready."

"But," O'Ryan said, turning to her twin, "how

can they possibly say that about us this year? At ten, we're going to be *way* old enough!"

"Yeah, but it's not like you guys are going to be turning eleven—like Yvette and me," Vanessa replied smugly.

Yvette nodded and smiled at Vanessa. "Yep. Turning eleven *is* a whole 'nother level."

"'Cause when you turn eleven that means you're practically thir*teen*."

"But!" Gwen smiled. "Even though you guys are only turning ten—like I'm going to be at my next birthday, and Oki, too—I'm *sure* your parents think you're mature enough to handle a dog now!"

"Really?" Reese asked. "You really think so?"

"Definitely," Gwen said, and was just about to add that she was a-thousand-million-times totally sure, but stopped herself when she saw Vanessa raise her eyebrows at her, and Yvette shake her head.

"It's not good to get their hopes up, Gwen," Vanessa scolded.

"And making them think their parents will let them get a dog is *not* a very mature thing to do," Yvette added.

"Hey, lay off! Gwen was just trying to make the twins feel better," Oki said, jumping up from her chair to make the point.

But when Oki pulled out her chair, she forgot something…she forgot about her egg baby.

And in just that instant, it started to roll…

"Nooooooo!" Oki yelled, frozen to the spot as she pictured her egg baby turning into Humpty Dumpty!

But just before the egg crashed to the floor, Gwen dove for it.

"Got him!" Gwen cried out.

"Oh, thanks!" Oki said, taking her egg baby back from Gwen and stroking its shell. "That was a close call."

"I guess you'll know to be more careful next time," Vanessa said to Oki.

"Yeah," Yvette nodded. "You'll learn."

Oki looked at the two older girls and narrowed

her eyes. "Just because you guys are in fifth grade doesn't mean you know everything!"

"Well, obviously we're mature enough to know how to take care of an egg baby better than you," Vanessa responded.

Uh-oh.

"Hey! Hey! Girls!" Gwen said quickly, hoping to break the tension. "We're upsetting the eggs. And Oki," Gwen said, using a  pretend grown–up voice, "the older girls didn't mean any harm. 'Cause seriously, how could anyone think we're immature?" And as she said this, Gwen put an enormous orange rind between her lips.

Then she gave a big orangutan smile.

Reese started laughing first.

Then O'Ryan.

A moment later, Oki couldn't help it: She was giggling, too.

Then both Vanessa and Yvette joined in—how could they not?

And before they knew it, all the Groovy Girls were laughing together like happy little monkeys!

Chapter 4
The Worst Best Idea

"I have the best idea!" Reese said as the twins walked home from soccer practice that afternoon.

"If you're gonna say that we should do extra homework today so we won't have any on our birthday weekend, don't!" O'Ryan replied.

"Nooo!" Reese said, rolling her eyes. "I'm talking about doing something to earn us a puppy!"

"Oh, okay, I'm listening," O'Ryan replied.

"I think we should show Mom and Dad that we're 'responsible citizens.' 'Cause if we can do

that, I bet they'd give us permission to get a dog."

"Wow," O'Ryan responded, "that actually *is* a good idea! What should we do?"

"Well, we could repaint Mom and Dad's bedroom," Reese suggested.

"With what?" O'Ryan asked.

"We've got a lot of glitter nail polish—it could be really pretty," Reese said.

"Oh! *Or*," O'Ryan said excitedly, "maybe we could get Dad a new car from eBay?!"

"That would be superrific!"

By now the twins had reached home, and they stopped to bang out their cleats, which were caked in mud, before going in. Mom hated getting mud tracks on the floor, so the girls wanted to be sure to clean their shoes off really, really well today. But first, they put their backpacks down *ver-ry care-fully* because their eggs were in them.

"Hey, do you think there's something we can do tonight—like at dinner—to show them we're responsible?" O'Ryan asked Reese.

"Tonight's spaghetti night, isn't it? So, why don't we make dinner?"

"Yeah! We could totally do that," O'Ryan exclaimed. "We've watched Mom make spaghetti every Thursday for practically our whole lives!"

But when the girls got to the kitchen, Mom was already mid-spaghetti prep.

"We're here to help!" Reese said.

"Really? How fabulous!" Mom replied. Then she added, "But I can tell you, your birthday presents aren't hidden in the kitchen cabinets."

"We know that already!" Reese responded.

"Yeah, we looked in them yesterday," O'Ryan said, so only her twin could hear. But then she added, "See, Reese and I want to help because, you know, the two of us are getting older. And we're, like, *very* responsible now."

"Okay." Mom smiled. "Good to know."

"I'm gonna set the table and make it really nice," Reese exclaimed, climbing up on the counter.

But when Mom saw Reese grabbing Grandma's fine china, she gasped. "You know what?" Mom said quickly. "Let's just use our regular plates tonight."

"Oh, okay," Reese said, jumping back down.

"I'll stir the sauce!" O'Ryan cried out, taking the wooden spoon from the drawer. "And now, some music to cook by!" She banged the spoon on the counter until she reached the pot. Then she began stirring with great gusto.

Problem was, O'Ryan's gusto was *much more robust-o* than the sauce in the pot.

And by stirring so *strongly*, she caused a tidal wave of tomato matter.

Sauce splattered EV-ER-Y-WHERE.

It got on the countertop.

It got on O'Ryan's shirt.

And some even splashed on O'Ryan's bangs!

"Good thing you've got red hair," Mom said, trying not to laugh when she saw the mess.

"Yeah," O'Ryan said. Normally something like this would have made her laugh, too. But she didn't think giggling would make her sound very *responsible*—which would only make their puppy-getting-permission-slip mission even harder.

"O'Ryan, you're planning to clean that up, aren't you?" Reese quickly asked. But Reese wasn't *really* asking. It was more like she was *telling* her sister to clean up the mess.

"You bet I'm going to clean it up," O'Ryan replied. "I'm very responsible like that," she added glancing over at her mother.

"Know what, Mom?" Reese said. "I think we have this under control. So why don't you go rest now? O'Ryan and I will call you and Dad to dinner when everything's ready."

"And we'll make a salad, too!" O'Ryan added.

"Okay," Mom replied. "I'll just drain the spaghetti and put it in a bowl. And you guys can bring it to the table when everything else is ready."

"Thanks, Mom!" both girls said together.

"You're welcome," Mom said, amused by the two helpful workers who had replaced her daughters. "And thank *you*!"

After O'Ryan and Reese finished setting the kitchen table together—and threw lettuce on some plates for salad— they were ready.

"COME 'N GET IT!" O'Ryan shouted.

"O'Ryan!" Reese scolded. "Don't do it like that. You need to make it sound *adult-i-er*."

But their folks must have been ready because they came running in to the kitchen anyway!

"I hear I'm in for quite a treat," Dad said, smiling at the twins.

"You just sit down, Dad, and we'll serve you!" O'Ryan replied.

"Yeah," Reese said. "Just leave it to your supreme servers. We can take care of everything!"

Both girls were *so* excited, they started fighting over who got to carry the spaghetti bowl to the table. (They forgot about the sauce.)

"I should take it," O'Ryan said. "I'm older."

"Only by seven minutes," Reese replied. "And, anyway, it was my idea to help!" Reese added, pushing her sister away.

"Reese, let go!" O'Ryan said.

"No, you!" Reese shouted back, pulling the bowl toward her.

"You!" said O'Ryan, grabbing it back.

"You!" replied Reese, holding on to its side.

As each girl pushed and pulled, the spaghetti decided it would get to the table all by itself.

The bowl went *flying*!

And with it, each and every strand of spaghetti hit the floor.

"Smooth move, O'Ryan," Reese whispered.

"Real responsible, Reese," O'Ryan whispered right back.

"Uh, but don't worry, Mom and Dad!" Reese added quickly. "We'll get this mess cleaned up in a jiff."

"Yeah, 'cause that's how responsible we are!" O'Ryan said, smiling with all her teeth.

"Why don't I just throw some burgers on the grill in the meantime," Dad said, since the spaghetti dinner was all but over. He was trying hard not to laugh. Mom too. They both actually thought the whole thing was pretty funny, but they didn't want the girls to be upset.

"I can pat the meat into burger shapes," O'Ryan said.

"Know what, girls?" Mom replied with a smile. "I think you've *both* helped enough for one night!"

Reese looked at O'Ryan, and O'Ryan looked at Reese. And both girls knew exactly what the other was thinking: *WE BLEW IT! We were completely irresponsible!*

The burgers grilled quickly, so no one starved for *too* long. But even though the girls both loved Dad's hamburgers, that night neither one could finish her meal.

"We messed up big-time," Reese said to O'Ryan as she put the leftovers back into the fridge after dinner. "We were crazy kitchen klutzes."

"Yeah," O'Ryan replied, "we'll never get that puppy for our birthday now."

"Wow, and look at this!" Mom said, coming back into the kitchen. "You girls are even cleaning up? Without being asked?!"

The girls nodded.

"Well, this is a nice surprise! And speaking of surprises, I was going to keep *this* under wraps, but on Saturday—which, I believe, just also happens to be your birthday—we'll be going on a road trip with your friends."

"Really?" Reese said, instantly brightening.

"Where are we going?" O'Ryan asked excitedly.

"Well, I can't tell you *that*!" Mom replied, smiling. "That would ruin the surprise, wouldn't it?" Then she added, "You'll just have to wait till Saturday to find out."

"A surprise road trip?" O'Ryan repeated to Reese when the girls were alone.

"What do you think we're gonna do?" Reese asked.

"I don't know. But I think I know how we can figure it out!" O'Ryan said. "Back to the list!"

The twins took their egg babies, which had been sitting quietly on the counter, and ran upstairs. After they rested the eggs on their desks, Reese grabbed a notepad and a pencil. On the notepad she made three lists.

"I think London!" said O'Ryan.

"I think France!" said Reese.

Likely places to go on a road trip

Places it would be groovy to go on a road trip

Places I've always dreamed of going on a road trip, but might take a plane to get to

O'Ryan really was trying to act mature, but enough was enough, and she decided she needed a break from maturity. So she couldn't help adding, "I think I see your underpants!"

Chapter 5

A Loo-Loo of a Surprise

"So, do you know how long it's gonna take to get to Rinky Dink Junction?" Gwen asked Reese as the two friends played at the McCloud's the next day after school—just one day before the twins' birthday.

Reese had just told Gwen that she'd heard about the birthday road trip.

"Rinky Dink Junction?" Reese repeated. "So *that's* where we're going, huh?"

Gwen instantly realized her mistake. And she worried she'd just blown the surprise.

"Rinky Dink Junction?" Gwen replied, panicking. "Uh, no. We're not going there. Why would you think that?" Gwen hoped if she denied it, maybe Reese would forget what she had said.

"I'm asking because you JUST SAID that's where we're going!" Reese smiled. "Oh, I can't wait to tell Mom and Dad I found out where we're going."

"Please, no!" Gwen cried. "You can't. You can't tell anyone I told you about going to Rinky Dink."

"Why not?"

"'Cause nobody thinks I can keep a secret. And if you tell them I told you, that'll just prove them right." Gwen shook her head.

When Reese realized Gwen wasn't kidding, she said, "All right, I promise not to tell anyone—except O'Ryan, okay?"

"Thanks, babe!" Gwen said, hugging her friend.

Reese hugged Gwen right back, then ran upstairs to find her sister. And as soon as Reese spilled Gwen's info, O'Ryan went directly to the computer.

"So, let's find out what we're going to see in Rinky Dink," O'Ryan exclaimed, clapping her hands.

Gwen bit her nails as O'Ryan typed, nervous about what the girls might find on the screen. But Gwen saw that there was some good news (at least at first) because O'Ryan turned out to be as bad a speller as she was!

"R-I-N-K-E-E D-O-N-K," O'Ryan pecked on the keyboard.

No Results for Rinkee Donk, the monitor read.

"It's not Rinkee Donk, it's Rinky Dink, you ding-a-ling," Reese said, pushing O'Ryan right off the keyboard. "World Wide Web, don't fail me now," Reese added after she'd correctly typed in the name of the town.

The first link that came up was for an Irish rock band.

"That can't be it," O'Ryan said.

Next one was for an apron-making company in Ohio. "Nope, that's not it, either," Reese added.

Then...pay dirt!

Link number three was an entry for Large Lou's Museum of Loo-Loos, located at Rinky Dink Junction in the town of Rinky Dink!

"What in the world is Large Lou's Museum of Loo-Loos?" Reese asked as she clicked on the link.

"Welcome to Large Lou's Museum of Loo-Loos!" a voice boomed through the computer speakers. "Located in the heart of Rinky Dink, right at the junction, our museum features the World's Largest Stuff EVER!"

The pictures on the site showed a twenty-foot-tall papier-mâché gorilla standing next to a ten-foot-tall banana.

There was a gigantic roller skate, too.

And a HUGE can of spray cheese.

Then the computer voice started speaking again.

"And remember, moms and dads, Large Lou's Museum of Loo-Loos is a great place to host a birthday party for your kids! Little ones love it!"

"Holy cow!" Reese said.

"They're throwing us a kiddie party at Large Lou's?!" O'Ryan asked Gwen in disbelief.

"Uh," Gwen said, biting her lip. "You can't make me say any more! Believe whatever you want. But just remember, I didn't tell you an-y-thing!"

"We know," Reese replied, sounding supremely

disappointed. "I just can't believe that *this* is what Mom and Dad think of us. They still think we're little kids who want a little-kiddie party!"

"Aw, come on," Gwen giggled. "You have to admit that can of spray cheese *is* kind of fun."

"But that's not the point!" Reese said.

"The *point*," O'Ryan continued, finishing her twin's thought, "is that if Mom and Dad think this is what we'd like, they don't think we're very mature."

"And if they don't think we're mature," Reese continued, "they don't think we're responsible."

"And if they don't think we're responsible," O'Ryan added, "they won't agree to let us get one of Mrs. Pearlman's puppies."

"Oh," Gwen nodded. "I get your drift now."

"We've got to make them change their minds about this somehow," O'Ryan said.

"Maybe we could just drop hints about how much we hope we're not going to a dumb museum," Reese replied. "So they'll know we wouldn't want to go to one."

"No, that won't work. That'll just make us seem even younger," O'Ryan said. "'Cause old people actually like ALL kinds of museums."

"She's right," Gwen replied. "Old people are mad for museums."

Okay. Think. Think. Think.

"Wait!" O'Ryan exclaimed. "What if we use this to our advantage?"

"What are you talking about?" Reese asked.

"What if we go along with the idea? Make believe we think going to a stupid museum is the greatest thing in the world."

"Why would we do that?"

"Because, little sister, mature people pretend to like things they don't like *all the time*!"

"But that's kind of like lying, isn't it?" Reese replied.

"Totally. Which is very mature!" O'Ryan assured her twin. "I mean, you know how Dad always says he loves Grandma's meatloaf, and we really know he hates it?"

"Oh, yeah!" Reese nodded, suddenly understanding. "And like Mom told Uncle Ben she thought his new tie was really nice, when we knew she thought it was tacky!"

"And she was right about that!" O'Ryan laughed.

"So what are you guys going to do?" Gwen asked.

"We're going to start playing along," Reese said.

"We're going to pretend to be really surprised and really happy that we're going to this silly museum for our birthday," O'Ryan nodded.

"Man," Reese exclaimed, "I'm feeling older and wiser already!"

O'Ryan walked to the mirror over her bureau. "A gigantic gorilla, how splendid!" she said, practicing her "surprise" face.

"Why, yes. How absolutely deee-lightful!" Reese added, joining O'Ryan at the mirror. "A giant can of spray cheese is what I call fine art!"

As maturely as possible, the twins smiled at each other's reflection.

Who knew "acting" mature could be so easy and so much fun!

"HA-PPY B-DAY!" Oki said excitedly to O'Ryan and Reese Saturday morning.

After 364 days of waiting, it was Reese and O'Ryan's birthday at last.

HA-PPY B-DAY!" Gwen yelled as she ran up the walkway a little later. "I woulda been here sooner, but I forgot Eggsmerelda, and I had to go back home and get her."

Gwen put her egg baby down and hugged Reese. Oki did the same—but hugged O'Ryan.

Then the huggers switched.

"So how does it feel to be double digits?" Oki asked.

"Superrific!" O'Ryan replied.

"Fanta*bulous*," Reese said, as their parents joined them. "As a matter of fact, as soon as O'Ryan woke up today I could see that she looked *even more* mature than she did yesterday!"

"Yeah," O'Ryan nodded, "and Reese looked much more responsible to me. But that's what being ten's all about!"

"Okay, you guys ready to go?" Reese asked.

"Well, we have to wait for Vanessa and Yvette, don't we?" Oki said.

"Actually, they're not going to be coming with us," O'Ryan replied.

"Why not?" Oki asked, crossing her arms.

"Well, when Vanessa called to wish us a happy birthday," O'Ryan said, "she told us that she and Yvette had some other stuff to do today."

"Oh," Oki said, shaking her head.

She couldn't believe it! Vanessa and Yvette had flaked. And Oki just bet it had something to do with that lunch on Thursday—when the fifth grade friends said how much more *mature* they were than the fourth graders.

"Well, you know what?" Gwen replied. "It's just too bad that those girls are going to be missing out on our fun. I mean, look!" Gwen said, holding up a picnic basket that she'd brought.

"Food for the road!" Oki explained. "Sticky-sweet breakfast stuff!"

"Oh, that's so supreme of you guys," Reese said.

"Well, let's get going," O'Ryan said.

As soon as they hopped in the car and were on their way, the girls broke out their sweet treats.

"Gwen, your cinnamon buns are scrump-dilly-umptious!" Reese said, licking her lips.

"Tank you veddy much!" Gwen replied crunching down on a handful of cereal. "And I love the way Oki put five different kinds of cereal in these lunch bags she decorated for us."

The girls crunched and munched and munched and crunched till they'd stuffed themselves silly.

After much chatting, many games of I Spy, and what seemed like *hundreds* of rounds of singing "Ninety-Nine Bottles of Pop on the Wall," a big billboard came into view on the side of the road.

"Welcome to Rinky Dink," O'Ryan read. "Home of Large Lou's Museum of Loo-Loos."

"Gee," Reese said, trying her best to seem surprised, "that sounds interesting! Doesn't it, O'Ryan?"

"Sure does," O'Ryan replied. "What's that?" she added, pointing to the giant gorilla and hamming it up.

"Looks like great art!" Reese replied.

Gwen couldn't help herself—she started giggling. And she laughed even harder at the surprised looks on the twins' faces when the car sped right past Large Lou's Museum of Loo-Loos!

"Huh?" O'Ryan replied. "What's going on?"

And both girls were even more confused when the car finally stopped in the driveway of an old farmhouse.

"Look at all the hay!" Gwen shouted.

Then, suddenly, it dawned on Reese why their parents had brought them to a place like this...and it was worse than she ever could have imagined! Worse even than the kiddie party they had mistakenly expected at Large Lou's Museum of Loo-Loos.

"Hay rides?!" she said, with undisguised disappointment. "We're going on hay rides?!"

Even though Reese and O'Ryan wanted to play it cool, the idea that their parents thought they'd like something like this—something even more babyish than a party at Loo-Loos—was just too much!

"Aren't we a bit old for hay rides?" O'Ryan asked.

"Hey, what's wrong with hay rides?" Gwen said.

"Yeah, I think they're fun, too," Oki added.

"Well, it's just that we didn't think we'd be doing them on our birthday," Reese said, trying to regain her fast-fading sense of maturity.

"Hay rides?" Mom said, turning around to face the girls. "Who said anything about hay rides?"

"Yeah," Dad replied, "maybe you girls should just hop out of the car and see what the rest of this farm has to offer."

"Okay," O'Ryan said, unbuckling her seat belt and opening the door.

"I'm just gonna stay in the car," Gwen said. "So you can leave your egg babies here with me."

Reese looked at Gwen, but before she had time to say anything, she heard a loud barking sound. Then a very friendly copper-colored dog trotted out from behind the barn to greet her. It was a gorgeous golden retriever!

"Well, hello, doggy!" Reese said, petting the dog's lustrous long fur.

Oki and O'Ryan quickly joined Reese. And that's when the girls got their next surprise.

Ruff-ruff-ruff-ruff-ruff-ruff-ruff.

Pound-pound-pound-pound-pound.

Bark-bark-bark-bark-bark.

The sound of forty little puppy feet came rumbling toward them. And all those feet, attached to ten different puppies, crashed to a halt right next to the big mommy dog.

"Look at all these doggies!" O'Ryan said, as the girls thrilled at the sight of the playful pups.

"Yes, there usually are a lot of dogs at a puppy farm," Mom replied, smiling.

Reese and O'Ryan looked at each other. A puppy farm? The girls had heard of a horse farm. And a cow farm. And a chicken farm. But they'd never heard of a puppy farm...

And why would their parents have brought them to a puppy farm on their birthday?

"Girls," Dad said, "Mom and I have been amazed by how responsible you've become."

"You mean 'cause of the dinner we tried to make the other night?" Reese asked.

"Nope." Mom shook her head. "Not just because of that. But because of the little things you've been doing each and every day. Like helping to clear the table without being asked. Like taking care not to muddy up the rugs. Like even cleaning up our bedroom better than Dad and I had had it. For all those reasons, we think both of you have proven you're ready for a dog."

"Wait a minute!" Reese exclaimed. "So you're not joking? You're saying that we're really here to get a dog? Not just to *play* with them?"

"And you're saying that we've *earned* it?" O'Ryan added.

Mom and Dad nodded.

O'Ryan and Reese's mouths dropped open.

"REALLY?"

"Yes, really!" Dad said, a puppy nipping at his cuff.

The girls grabbed each other's hands and started jumping up and down. Which caused the puppies to get even more excited, turning them into a blur of yelping, panting, wagging fur!

"Wait!" Dad yelled. "Could you guys do that little dance again? My camcorder wasn't on yet!" But the girls didn't even have to be asked because they weren't going to stop dancing around any time soon!

"Ohmigosh! Look at how playful she is. We have to get this one!" O'Ryan said, petting one of the puppies.

But Reese had already picked up one of the other little ones. "No way, look at him. This guy's the most adorable thing I've ever seen." She tickled the puppy's belly, and the dog immediately started licking her face.

"No, mine's better!" O'Ryan insisted. She also couldn't help but notice that the puppy in her hands didn't seem to like Reese at all.

"Nuh-uh, mine!" Reese shouted right back. (Reese's dog had no interest in O'Ryan, either.)

"Maybe they can get *both*?" Oki asked, looking for a way to solve the problem.

"No, I'm sorry, girls, we can absolutely only take one," Mom answered.

"Well, then we should get mine. I'm older!" O'Ryan said.

"So what?" Reese replied.

"Guys," Oki said, "I think the maturity factor is dipping here."

Speaking of maturity, with all the excitement, everyone had forgotten about paying attention to Gwen.

Gwen, who was still sitting in the car with her seat belt on.

Mom knocked on one of the car windows, which was open just a tiny little bit. "Gwen, don't you want to come out and play with the puppies?"

Gwen shook her head. "No, thanks, I'm good. Besides, someone has to watch the egg babies."

Reese walked over to Mom and whispered, "Gwen's a little afraid of dogs."

"Oh." Mom nodded. "Well, maybe you could show her through the window how cuddly and friendly the puppies are. Puppies can sometimes seem a lot less scary than full-grown dogs."

"Yeah!" Reese said. "Hey, girls," she called to the others. "Let's show Gwen how nice-'n-not-scary these puppies are."

Oki and O'Ryan rushed over to the car, each carrying a squirmy little pup in her arms.

The dog in O'Ryan's arms looked like it was trying to lick Gwen's face clear through the window! And Gwen had to admit that holding that little doggy looked like it would be a lot of fun.

Reese's puppy wasn't moving around all that much—he just looked kind of tired. And sure enough, a minute later, he stretched out his paws and gave the cutest little puppy yawn you could imagine!

"He looks like me at the beginning of the school day!" Gwen exclaimed.

When Reese's puppy closed his brown eyes, Gwen rolled down her window some more.

"Do you think maybe I could pet him?" she asked.

"I think he'd like that a lot," Reese replied.

Gwen put her hand out, a little nervously at first, and stroked the dog's head as Reese held him.

"He's the softest thing I've ever touched!" Gwen said.

"I think he likes you," Reese replied. "Do you want to hold him?"

Gwen didn't say anything for a moment. She just stared at the sleepy little pup.

"Oki," Gwen finally said. "Do me a favor?"

"Sure," Oki replied.

"Could you watch the egg babies for a minute? I want to get out of the car to hold the puppy."

When Gwen took the puppy from Reese, O'Ryan suddenly realized that she could be very happy with that dog, too.

He was cuddly. He was friendly. He was quiet.

O'Ryan looked at Reese and smiled, and her seven-minutes-younger twin smiled right back.

After they'd talked to the breeder and officially bought that pup, along with a collar and leash, and a crate for him to sleep and travel in, the McClouds put the puppy in the back of the station wagon.

"So," Oki said to the twins, "what are you going to name him?"

"Henry," Reese said.

"Nuh-uh," O'Ryan replied, "he's totally a Max."

"No, he's not!"

"Yes, he is!"

And as the two *very mature* McCloud twins kept bickering all the way home, their now fully awake, frisky new puppy—whatever his name was—happily barked along with them!

Chapter 7

Party Pooper!

"SURRRRRPRRRRISSSSE!" Reese and O'Ryan heard as they turned the knob to their front door.

"AAAHHHHH!" screamed the two VERY surprised twins.

"RUFFRUFFRUFF!" barked their over-excited new puppy.

"Happy surprise slumber party!" Yvette shouted, as she and Vanessa threw confetti at the girls.

While the others had been at the puppy farm, Vanessa and Yvette had stayed back to decorate the McClouds' house with paw-print balloons, puppy-wrapping-papered presents, and streamers.

The puppy ran around in little puppy circles, and then, without warning, *peed on the floor*!

"I think he needs to go outside," Reese said.

"I think it's a little late for that," O'Ryan responded. "Let's get something to clean up the puddle."

But when the girls walked into the kitchen, they got another not-so-little surprise!

Yvette's mom was holding a cake in the shape of a dog bone, brightly lit with ten candles and an extra candle for good luck!

"Happy birthday, girls!" Yvette's mom said as everyone broke out into a loud chorus of "Happy Birthday."

"Holy cow!" Reese exclaimed.

"Ohmigosh!" O'Ryan beamed.

As the twins approached the cake, their new puppy jumped around at their heels.

"Okay," O'Ryan said, "on the count of three."

"One," said Reese.

"Two," said O'Ryan.

"THREE!" the girls said. Then, closing their eyes to make their wishes, they blew out the candles.

Reese laughed when she opened her eyes. "I didn't even *know* what to wish for," she said.

"I mean, I already *got* exactly what I wanted!"

"I'd say that makes you a pretty lucky girl," Mom replied.

"Of course she's lucky," O'Ryan said. "She has *me* as an older sister."

"And *me* as a best friend," Gwen added.

"And *me* as a fashion consultant!" Oki smiled, flipping up Reese's collar.

"And *us* as super-duper party planners!" Vanessa chimed in.

"Which makes our puppy pretty lucky, too!" Reese said.

"Yeah, and I think he should be an honorary member of the Groovy Girls," O'Ryan nodded. "He'll be our group egg baby—only a real one!"

"With two mommies and four new aunties," Reese added.

The dog must have liked the idea, because he started running back and forth across the kitchen floor between them, slipping and sliding on the tiles.

"He's soooo precious," Vanessa said. "What are you going to call him?"

"Henry!" said Reese.

"Max!" said O'Ryan.

"I think you should call him Lacey," Yvette said.

"But Lacey's a girl's name. Why would they

want to call him that?" Gwen asked.

"'Cause look!" Yvette replied, pointing to the dog, who was now busy chewing the shoelaces on the pile of sneakers by the kitchen door.

"Puppy, no!" Reese yelled.

The puppy looked back at her with the saddest eyes and whimpered.

Reese felt terrible; she absolutely couldn't stay mad, so she changed her mind. "It's okay, you can chew the laces if you want," she said.

So much for parental discipline!

"Way to teach him a lesson, Reese!" O'Ryan said, shaking her head.

"Okay, *you* try punishing him then!"

O'Ryan looked at her new little puppy, who was happily chewing up her left sneaker. "That's okay," she said, laughing, "I need new kicks, anyway!"

"Come on, girls. Let's go back into the living room. The party's just starting!" Yvette said. "And what would our sleepovers be without PIZZA?!"

The girls made a beeline to the living room so they could have their cake—and eat pizza, too!

"Doggy, please!" Gwen said, trying to chew her slice while the puppy, who she had put in her lap, licked her face.

"Look at you, Gwen!" Reese said to her friend, proudly.

"I just think he's hungry," O'Ryan said, pulling a slice of pizza from the box and dangling it above the puppy. "Here ya go, Max. Jump!"

"Jump, Henry!" Reese said.

And boy, oh boy, did that dog—whatever his name was—jump!

But after he'd ripped through his slice, he rolled on the ground. And then the pizza...well, let's just say the pizza came out the same way it went in!

"MOM!" O'Ryan called. "We have a PROB-lem!"

"Maybe giving him a slice wasn't such a good idea," Reese said.

When Mom came into the living room and saw how the puppy had "decorated" the floor, she nodded. "Well, it's a good thing you girls are so *responsible,* because I know you'll do a good job of cleaning up the puppy's mess."

"Ugh," the girls groaned.

"Yup," Mom said, "and you'll have to clean up after him when he pees again, probably in another minute. *This* is what owning a puppy is all about."

O'Ryan and Reese looked at each other and frowned. This was not exactly what the girls had in mind when they'd been dreaming of a doggy.

"The puppy puke is starting to smell," Vanessa said, fanning her nose.

"Well, since it is a special day, I'll do the honors this time," Mom replied, pointing to the mess. "Why don't you guys go outside for a little air."

"Thanks, Mom," Reese said.

"I'll get the leash," O'Ryan said.

As the girls walked outside with the dog, Vanessa turned to the twins. "So, were you guys really surprised by the party? Or did you know?"

"No, I had no idea!" O'Ryan answered.

"Me neither. I was supremely surprised!" Reese echoed. "I mean, I can't believe all you guys kept it secret from us."

"Well," Gwen smiled, "it really wasn't that hard since Oki and I didn't know about it, either."

"You *didn't*?" O'Ryan asked, turning to Oki.

"No," Oki said, sounding ticked. "But I *wish* I had."

"Well, we just thought it'd be better to keep it between us fifth graders," Yvette replied.

Oki's mouth dropped open. She was trying to stay cool—she hadn't wanted to believe Yvette and Vanessa were being age-snobs like they'd been at lunch the other day—but it seemed like they were.

"Are you kidding?" Oki said. "What does being older have to do with anything? I mean you can be a really mature nine-year-old and a really immature eleven-year-old. It's all about the person!"

"Yeah, but we know how hard it is keeping a secret from your best friends," Vanessa tried to explain, since everyone knew that Oki was O'Ryan's BFF and Gwen was Reese's.

"So we thought we'd just make it easier for you," Yvette added.

Remembering how she'd accidentally told Reese they were going to Rinky Dink, Gwen responded, "Well, to be honest, I might not have been able to keep the surprise party all to myself."

"But you didn't even give us the chance to blow it!" Oki replied. "You just made the decision for us, without even thinking about how that might have made us feel."

Hearing the commotion, the puppy started whimpering. He seemed pretty upset, too.

As the girls tried to calm the little dog down, Yvette took a moment to think about what Oki had just said, and she realized that if she'd been in the same position, she would have felt hurt, too.

"You know what, Oki?" Yvette said. "You're right. I wasn't thinking about how it might have made you feel. I was only thinking about the surprise, which wasn't very mature of *me*, was it?"

"Not really." Oki smiled, beginning to feel better that her friend was willing to admit her mistake. "But owning up to it *is* very mature of you."

Then the friends hugged—Yvette and Oki, Vanessa and Gwen. The puppy also let it be known that he was happy with the way things had turned out. And he showed this by peeing again (just as Mom had predicted)!

"Okay, enough of all this make-up stuff!" O'Ryan said, happy that her friends were friends again. "We've got stuff to do—like getting back to the house and getting on with the party!"

"Back to the *slumber* party!" Reese said.

"Back to Eggsmerelda!" Gwen shouted. "I left her in your fridge to keep her cool. You think she'll be all right in there?"

"Sure," O'Ryan replied. "Unless Dad got hungry…"

"Hey," Vanessa said when the girls were back inside, "you guys still haven't opened your presents!"

"More presents?" Reese asked. "This party keeps getting better and better."

So the girls ran upstairs to the twins' room where the great unwrapping fiesta began!

"Cool, a zebra-striped doggy bed!" Reese said, when she opened Yvette and Vanessa's gift.

"Rockin'," O'Ryan shouted when she saw the puppy-print jammies Gwen had gotten them.

"S-weet!" Both girls giggled when they opened Oki's gift—a bright yellow doggy raincoat with four little booties.

"These gifts are so groovy, girls!" Reese said.

"Thank you, thank you!" O'Ryan added.

And then another round of hugging took place.

"I don't know about you guys," Gwen said, after all the presents had been opened, "but it was such a big day today, I'm beat like a drum."

"I'm so glad you said that!" Yvette replied. "'Cause all the secret-keeping and the party-planning wiped me out, too."

"Well, girls, this is just a *suggestion*," Vanessa said, smiling, "but maybe we want to think about getting into our PJs and going to sleep."

"Now that sounds like a very *mature* idea." Oki nodded.

"Yeah! And let's bring the puppy's crate up here so he can sleep with us, too," O'Ryan suggested.

"Good thinking," Reese said.

But as soon as the girls turned the lights out, this is what they heard:

"AAAA-RRRRRUUUUUUUWWWWW!"

"Excuse me!" Gwen giggled. "Usually, my stomach doesn't rumble that loud."

Reese turned on the light, and she saw the puppy standing at attention in his crate.

"Okay, doggy, it's *really* time for bed," O'Ryan said, patting the dog's paws. Then she flipped off the light switch.

"AAAA-RRRRRUUUUUUUWWWWW!" the dog went again. Followed by, "AAAA-RRRRUUUWWW!" and then, "AAAA-RRRRRUUUUUUUWWWWW!"

But no matter what the girls did—taking the dog out of the crate, holding and petting him, or giving him a chew toy—their new pup kept whimpering.

Funnily enough, much like the other Groovy Girls at their first sleepover, their newest (four-legged) member decided he wanted to stay awake ALL NIGHT LONG.

"Okay, doggy!" Vanessa said at 1:30 in the A.M. "Really, now it's time to lie down and go to sleep."

"AAAA-RRRRRUUUUUUUWWWWW!" the puppy howled in response.

And at 2:15 A.M., just as Yvette had started dozing off again: "AAAA-RRRRRUUUUUUUWWWWW!"

By 5:17, Oki's eyes were burning from being open so long. "Puppy, what are you trying to do to us?" she asked.

But it seemed like the answer was pretty clear: He was trying to help them stay awake ALL NIGHT, just like they'd once *thought* they wanted to do.

At 8:30 A.M. when the girls finally gave up on sleeping, they trooped downstairs to get some breakfast.

"Well," O'Ryan said, "thanks to our new doggy, Groovy Girls Slumber Party Number Three turned out to be the first official No-Sleep Sleepover Party we'd ever had!"

"Yeah, thanks a lot, puppy," Gwen said, not sounding very thankful.

"Good news is," Reese nodded, "now that we've done it, we'll NEVER have to do it again!"

And all the Groovies couldn't have agreed more!

What My Egg Baby Taught Me

By: Reese McCloud

This Responsible Citizen project taught me that being responsible for something is hard. It taught me that having to take care of an egg is hard. And it taught me that when an egg hits the floor, it doesn't stay hard!...Just kidding.

But, I learned something else, too. I learned Gwen is one of the most responsible citizens I know. She not only takes great care of an egg, but she takes great care of her friends, too.

Even though she was scared of dogs, she came to the puppy farm on my birthday because she knew how much it would mean to me. And because she was willing to check it out, she learned that some dogs aren't really scary at all!

I know now that having a puppy is a lot of work. In fact, O'Ryan and I named our new puppy "Sleepless." (Did I mention that he doesn't like to sleep through the night?) Anyway, a dog needs someone who is kind, loving, and responsible. So that's why I think Gwen should get a Pearlman Puppy. Because I can't imagine any pup being doggone luckier than to get Gwen as an owner!

Groovy Girls™
sleepover handbook

SENSATIONAL SURPRISES & BIRTHDAY BASHES:
Great Ideas for **SUPER CELEBRATIONS**

Ready for a
FOUR-LEGGED FRIEND?
find out if you're pet-perfect

Super-Sized Stuff

You're in for Some **BIG-TIME** Fun

Contents

Text by Julia Marsden
Illustrations by Yancey Labat, Bill Alger, Kurt Marquart

A Groovy Greeting

HI, GROOVY GIRL!

Guess what?! The Groovies are planning a surprise sleepover party for you and your friends!

Uh-oh—I did it again!

When it comes to super-spectacular celebrations—like surprise birthday parties—I just can't seem to keep my lips sealed! Well, that's okay, because now that I let you in on our little secret, I can share with you all our totally terrific ideas, games, and delish recipes (which are great fun, whether you're celebrating a birthday or not).

Inside you'll find ways to surprise your BFF all day long.

Does she like snooping around for birthday presents (like a certain pair of twins I know)? Then turn to page 6 to plan a scavenger-hunt adventure.

Maybe you'd like to invite a few furry friends to your party! You'll be feeling the puppy love (and kitty, hamster, and birdie love, too) in no time with all kinds of purrrrr-fect pets! See pages 8–10.

And what would a party be without some yummy-licious treats?! Turn to pages 12–14 for super-duper desserts and snacks like dog-bone cookies and cupcake critters to serve at your surprise sleepover. Mmmmmm, just talking about these goodies is making me hungry! (Is it lunchtime yet?)

Now, there's only one prob—how are you going to keep all these splenderrific secrets and surprises all to yourself? Well, page 7 should give you some tips, and if you're anything like me—lots of "oops's" and "sorry's" and "I didn't really just say that's" will help, too!

See you again soon, groovy girl! And keep this just between us, okay?

Kisses and hugs,
Gwen*

Planning special surprises for a friend on her birthday can be a piece of cake! Why not start by making plans for a birthday sleepover like the Groovies do? You can let everyone in on the "reason" for the get-together except the birthday girl!

🎁 After she's opened her birthday presents, create an outfit made from the gift wrap, bows, and ribbons for her to wear. Fashion a belt with ribbons and accessorize with a bow. A gift bag can make a happening handbag!

🎁 Beat the birthday girl to the bathroom in the morning and write a birthday message on the bathroom mirror using a dry-erase pen. (Be sure to get her parents' permission first!)

If your friend's birthday is during the week:

1. Give her a birthday bagel, muffin, doughnut, or cupcake with a birthday candle stuck in it when you meet up in the morning at school.

2. Give small gifts (like stickers, candy bars, or fun pencils) throughout the day that total the number of years the birthday girl will be celebrating. Or give her a homemade gift, like a batch of cookies, or a birthday coupon book (see page 11).

3. Tie balloons to her locker or desk at school.

Pooch-y Keen Party Planner

you love animals as much as the twins do, why not unleash
party that's a real canine caper! Consider these cool ideas...

ut together a party playlist or look for a compilation CD
hat includes songs like:

* Who Let the Dogs Out? *Baha Men*
* You Ain't Nothing But a Hound Dog *Elvis Presley*
* (How Much Is That) Doggy in the Window *Patti Page*
* Me and You and a Dog Named Boo *Kent LaVoie*

tage a dance contest by having guests create a dance that they
each everyone else. The guest who best "trains" the others with
er dance tricks is the winner. Also, play your tunes or use them
s the music that stops when you play Hot Dog (see below).

erve tasty treats such as Pups in a Blanket (wrap hot dogs in
rescent-roll dough and bake until the dough is golden), and a
nunchy, crunchy snack like People Chow (see page 13). Then let
ach guest decorate her own cute cupcake critters (see page 14).

each an old dog new tricks with this variation
n the traditional party game below!

Hot Dog
What You Do:

lay this game—a variation of Hot Potato—by passing around
stuffed animal puppy that's wrapped in multiple layers of
vrapping paper. Play some music from the pooch playlist above
nd, when the music stops, the girl holding the present gets to
nwrap a layer of paper. Start the music again and continue
assing the present. The girl who unwraps the last layer of
gift wrap gets to keep the stuffed pooch.

SURPRISE-PARTY SCAVENGER HUNT

Keep the excitement going with a scavenger hunt!

✳Decide on the number of players or teams and whether you're going to play inside or out (or a combo of both).

✳Players will search for items on a scavenger-hunt list you make ahead of time.

✳Working together or on their own, players search for the items on their lists. The items can be a combination of the stuff you hide for them to find, and easy-to-find stuff that you don't have to hide (like a multi-colored leaf or a lost button). No one should have to look through cupboards or drawers.

✳Let everyone know which areas of the house or yard are considered part of the hunt area.

Here's the type of list you can make for your birthday scavenger hunt:

1. A birthday candle
2. A piece of birthday wrapping paper
3. A birthday card

✳Set a time limit.

✳Award prizes to the person or team who finds everything on the list the fastest.

✳For a birthday-themed scavenger hunt, you can also write the word "HAPPY BIRTHDAY" or the birthday girl's name vertically down one side of a piece of paper. Then list objects that start with each letter that can be found in the area where the party is taking place. Here's an example using Reese's and O'Ryan's names.

Red crayon

Earring

Eraser

Spoon

Envelope

Oven mitt

Rubber band

Yarn

Apple

Nail file

Super-Secret Tips and Pet-Perfect Solutions

If you've got a secret that's too good to keep to yourself, or a secret wish for a pet of your own...read on! These helpful tips are made for you.

Pssst! I've Got a Secret!

My friends and I are planning a surprise birthday party for my BFF, but I'm finding it really hard to keep it a secret from her. I always feel like I'm about to spill the beans. What should I do?

It totally makes sense that you're having a tough time keeping this exciting info to yourself. After all, you and your BFF are probably used to sharing all kinds of secrets. When you feel like you're about to tell all, steer your conversation toward a sharable secret that you're both already in on. And if you're on the phone with her, stage a quick wrap-up of your talk and speed dial one of your friends who's in on the party planning. The two of you will be able to talk about the upcoming bash all you want without blowing the surprise.

Puppy Love

I really want a puppy. My parents keep telling me that having a pet is a lot of work. How can I prove to them that I'm ready for the responsibility?

There's way more to having a dog than feeding it treats and showing it off to your friends. As a responsible canine caretaker, your daily duties are going to include things such as feeding, walking, and grooming your pooch. Why not offer to take care of a neighbor's pet for a few days to show your parents how committed you are to caring for an animal of your own? Or let your parents know that you'll be taking care of an egg baby, sugar baby, or flour baby (a practice substitute for the real thing you'll be responsible for) for a week or more. Your actions are likely to go a long way toward showing them how responsible you can be when it comes to caring for a pet.

ANIMAL ANTICS

The Right Pet for You

Picking a pet can be both super-fun and exciting, but also a big responsibility! Want to know what pet might be right for you? Check out this info and see if you can make yourself a pet-perfect match!

Dogs

A dog can be a girl's best friend! Because canines can offer unconditional love and loyalty, it's easy to fall in love! Your pooch will be there for you as you leave for school each morning, and it'll be waiting happily for you at your doorstep when you return. Your pet will cuddle up next to you when you're sad, and listen to all you have to say. But with all this doggy love comes ha work and responsibility. Dogs need plenty of attention and time out—outside that is, for walks and exercise. For more about dog care and a list of some kid-friendly pooches, turn to page 10.

Overall care level: *High*

Cats

If you're looking for a cuddly companion who's also independent and less time-consuming than a dog (they don't need to be walked, after all!), then a cat may be the purrrrr-fect pet for you! Unlike dogs, cats don't need to be brought outside when they have to go to the bathroom—they ha a litter box indoors instead. And because they groom themselves : well, you won't need to comb their fur as much as a dog's, and y don't need to take them to the groomer's for a bath and haircut!

Overall care level: *Medium to high*

8

Birds

Some pets are for the birds! If you'd like a chirpy, feathered friend, who prefers a splash to a comb-out—then maybe a pet bird is for you! Cockatiels have very sweet personalities and soft voices. You can even teach them to speak a few words! Parakeets and finches like to be kept in pairs—so they're good at keeping themselves company. And if music is your thing, then a male canary is the right birdie match for you! When they're happy, they can sing beautiful melodies. **Overall care level:** *Medium*

Fish

Goldfish make a great first pet. They're pretty easy to take care of, and not very time-consuming. After all, they don't need to be cuddled, held, or taken outside for a walk! You'll need a fishbowl, which needs to be cleaned about once a week, and some fish food (it's important not to overfeed your fish—a pinch a day should do the trick!). Overall care level: *Low*

Hamsters

To keep a hamster happy, you need a cage (which should be cleaned once a week), a hamster wheel for exercise, a wooden chew toy so they won't gnaw on the cage bars (hamsters have small but sharp teeth!), a water bottle, and some hamster-mix food. While hamsters are furry, cute, and totally fun to play with, they're often up at night because they're nocturnal (which means they sleep during the day). So, unless you want to drift off to sleep to the sound of a squeaky hamster wheel, it's best to keep your furry friend in a room other than your bedroom. Other little pets that are in the same category as hamsters are mice, gerbils, and guinea pigs. **Overall care level:** *Medium*

BEST OF THE BREEDS

So, you're ready for a pooch pal and can't wait for the bark-o-rama fest to begin! What kind of dog should you get? Read on for facts and tips about finding the perfect canine companion for you and your family!

Big or Small—They're All Super-Duper Dogs!

Will you pick a pizzaz-zy big dog or a sensational small one? Big dogs (like golden retrievers and Labrador retrievers) need lots of room. If your home doesn't have a lot of open space, or your pet won't be given the run of the house, then you may want to choose a smaller dog (like a bichon frise or toy poodle).

Kid-friendly Canines

- If you'd like a kid-friendly gentle giant, consider: golden retrievers and Labrador retrievers.

- If you'd like a kid-friendly petite pooch, consider: pugs, toy poodles, and bichon frises.

- If you'd like a kid-friendly super-smart dog, consider: border collies and poodles.

- If you'd like a kid-friendly dog for the country, consider: spaniels, golden retrievers, and Labradors.

- If you'd like a kid-friendly dog for the city, consider: pugs and Boston terriers.

- If you want to give a home to a one-of-a-kind dog, consider a mixed-breed (mutt). Each dog has its own personality, but many mutts are very kid-friendly.

Eggs-tra Credit

While waiting for permissio[n] for a pup, try taking care [of] an egg baby!

To make an egg baby of your own, use colored markers to draw a face on an uncooked egg. For an added touch, glu[e] some yarn on the top of the egg for hair.

To make a sugar or flour baby decorate a plain piece of pape[r] with a face, and then wrap th[e] paper around a 5-pound bag of sugar or flour and tape it i[n] place. To really doll things up fit your sack with a small baby or doll outfit. Then top things off with a small baby bonnet!

A Fun–Filled Gift to Make for a
FRiEND'S BiRTHDAY

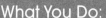

Birthday Coupon Book

Your friend's birthday is coming up and you want
to make her something that's one-of-a-kind special.
Create a coupon book that the birthday girl can turn
in to you at anytime, page by page, for all kinds of fun!

What You Do:

1. Trace the outline of your coupon
on colored construction paper or card
stock using a dollar bill as your guide.
Make as many pages for your book
as you like—a pack of ten coupons
makes a great gift!

2. Write out and decorate individual
coupons that say what they can be
redeemed—or traded in—for.
Some coupons can be for small treats, while others can be for
things that are truly priceless, or unique to your special friendship.

3. Once you've made all of the individual coupons, create a cover
and a message page that says something like: *This birthday coupon
book is my way of wishing you a happy birthday. These coupons
never expire and can be redeemed at any time.*

> ### What You Need:
> * Card stock or
>   construction paper
> * Colored pens
>   or markers
> * Stickers (optional)
> * Stapler

Here are some examples:

* A Manicure by Me in the
  Color of Your Choice
* Ice-Cream Run! A Double
  Scoop Ice-Cream Cone—
  My Treat!
* An Hour of Help with
  Your Chores

* Fabulous Free Phone Advice—
  All You Have to Do Is Call!
* A Batch of Homemade
  Cookies
* A Great Big Hug
* A Shoulder to Lean On

11

BONE APPETIT

If you're as much of a dog lover as Reese and O'Ryan, then you'll want to whip up these winning recipes for some delightful doggy-themed birthday desserts and snacks!

Doggone Delicious Sugar Cookies

Like the Groovy Girls, you probably know how sweet it can be to have a pup to play with. But when the munchies strike, throw a dog a bone and pick up one of these sweet treats for yourself!

Dog-Bone Cookies

(Makes about 3 dozen cookies)

Ingredients:

- 1/2 cup butter, softened
- 1 cup white sugar
- 2 eggs
- 1 teaspoon vanilla extract
- 2 1/2 cups all-purpose flour
- 1 teaspoon baking powder
- 1/2 teaspoon salt
- Rainbow sprinkles

Utensils: Measuring cups, measuring spoons, large mixing bowl, mixer, foil or plastic wrap, spatula, rolling pin, butter knife, cookie sheet

What else you need: A grown-up to help you

What You Do:

1. In a large mixing bowl, use a mixer to cream together the softened butter and sugar until smooth. Beat in the eggs and vanilla. By hand, stir in the flour, baking powder, and salt. Cover the bowl and chill in the fridge for at least one hour or overnight.

2. Have an adult preheat the oven to 400 degrees F. Roll out the dough on a floured surface so it's 1/4- to 1/2-inch thick. Cut into dog-bone shapes using your Dog Bone Cookie Cut-Out (see page 13) and a butter knife.

3. Decorate with sprinkles. Place the cookies one inch apart on an un-greased cookie sheet.

4. Have an adult place the cookie sheet in the preheated oven and bake the cookies for about 7 minutes. Cool completely.

og Bone Cookie Cut-Out

hat You Need:

Paper
Pencil
Tape
A small piece
of cardboard
or card stock
Scissors

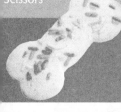

What You Do:

1. On a piece of paper, trace the dotted dog-bone outline at the top of the opposite page.

2. Cut out the dog-bone shape and tape it to the cardboard or card stock.

3. Cut out the dog-bone shape again, this time from the cardboard, and use this pattern and a butter knife to cut out your dog-bone cookies from the cookie dough. Or, you can use a dog-bone-shaped cookie cutter from a cooking supplies or crafts store.

eople Chow *(Makes about 5 cups)*

ble is cool for canines, but this crunchy
ck is sure to please the people in your life!

gredients:

up Corn Chex® cereal
up Rice Chex® cereal
up Wheat Chex®
ereal
up peanuts
r your favorite nut
cup raisins
nsils: Measuring
s, spoon, large
king bowl

What You Do:

1. Mix all ingredients together in a large mixing bowl.

2. Store in an airtight container or serve to your guests in personalized plastic dog bowls.

✳ Surprise Party People Chow!

You provide the peanuts and raisins. Then ask each of your party guests to bring one cup of her favorite unsweetened cereal in a zip-top plastic sandwich bag. When guests arrive, have them add what they brought to a large mixing bowl. Stir it up and then serve the snack that now has several surprise ingredients!

13

CUPCAKE CRITTERS

Give a plain cupcake a surprising finish with decorating details that turn an ordinary treat into something with animal appeal!

Lovable Lab

What You Need:

Chocolate frosting

Shredded coconut

Black shoestring licorice or black decorating icing

Small candies such as mini M&M's® or jelly beans, red fruit leather, or red decorating icing

What You Do:

Frost a cupcake with chocolate frosting. (Mix some shredded coconut into the frosting to create a furry coat.) Use black licorice string pieces or black decorating icing to create two floppy ears and mouth. Use small candies to create eyes and a nose. Flatten and curl a small piece of red fruit leather, or use red decorating icing, to create a tongue.

Cool Cat

What You Need:

* Frosting in your color of choice
* Small candies
* Black shoestring licorice
* Sugar wafer cookies or graham crackers

What You Do:

Frost a cupcake, and add small candies for eyes and a nose. Place short pieces of shoestring licorice near the nose for whiskers. Use a butter knife to cut a sugar wafer cookie or graham cracker into two small triangular pieces for ears. Add to the cupcake, and frost.

Funny Bunny

What You Need:

* Frosting in your color of choice
* Two peanut-shaped cookies such as Nutter Butters®
* Small candies

What You Do:

Frost a cupcake. Place two peanut-shaped cookies at the top of the cupcake to form rabbit ears. Frost the tops and sides of the cookies to match the rabbit face. Add eyes and a nose using small candies. Then make whiskers like you did for the cat.